alien
contact

alien contact

BOOK #5 OF THE
alien agent
series

Pamela F. Service

illustrated by
mike gorman

darbycreek
MINNEAPOLIS

For Alex and her newly Californian family
—P.S.

I'd like to dedicate this book right back to
Pamela F. Service. I've so enjoyed
illustrating your books!
—M.G.

Text copyright © 2010 by Pamela F. Service
Illustrations copyright © 2010 by Lerner Publishing Group, Inc.

Darby Creek
A division of Lerner Publishing Group, Inc.
241 First Avenue North
Minneapolis, MN 55401 U.S.A.

Website address: www.lernerbooks.com

Library of Congress Cataloging-in-Publication Data

Service, Pamela F.
        Alien contact / by Pamela F. Service ; illustrated by Mike Gorman.
            p.   cm. — (Alien agent ; #5)
        Summary: Zack, a human boy who is actually an extraterrestrial agent for the Galactic
Union, travels to California's Lassen Volcanic National Park on a dangerous mission to
save the Earth from evil aliens known as the Syndicate.
        ISBN: 978-0-7613-5363-8 (lib. bdg. : alk. paper)
        [1. Extraterrestrial beings—Fiction. 2. Lassen Volcanic National Park (Calif.)—
Fiction. 3. Science fiction.] I. Gorman, Mike, ill. II. Title.
PZ7.S4885An 2010
[Fic]—dc22   2009034766

Manufactured in the United States of America
1 – SB – 7/15/10

[aLien agent] series

Prologue

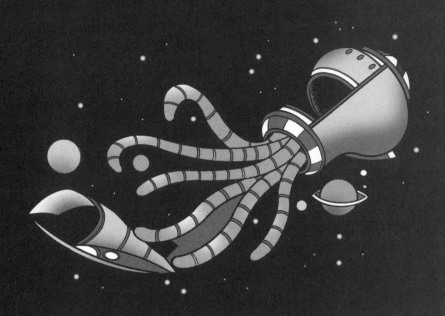

The alarm shrilled through the little spaceship. Agent Sorn spun around and stared at the screen. A ship was pursuing hers and closing in fast. Frowning, she studied the image. A Syndicate ship. Can't be good, she thought and accelerated full out.

Her pursuer was still closing the gap. Sorn bubbled with frustration.

Here she was on a routine mission to planet Earth. The job was so routine, in fact, that she had decided to handle it herself rather than bother their planted Alien Agent with it. She still felt guilty about how Agent Zack had been forced to learn about his real nature and take on dangerous missions before he'd had a chance to grow up, before he'd even been fully trained. Sorn had decided she'd handle this simple job herself and let Zack enjoy a little more time as an almost normal, human-seeming kid.

But suddenly things did not look routine. Her little ship was now going as fast as it could, but the other was still gaining. Grumbling, Sorn turned to her communicator. Quickly, she wrote a message to Galactic Union Headquarters: her coordinates, her mission, and (although she hated to do it) a call for help.

She jabbed the Send button just as a golden energy glow enveloped her ship. The enemy ship was grappling hers, pulling it in. Had her distress call gotten off in time?

Helplessly, Sorn watched as her ship lost power and the other moved in. Why, she asked herself yet again, did everything having to do with planet Earth cause so much trouble?

CHAPTER ONE

The space invaders' fleet blew up in a huge explosion. The hero and heroine stood on a hillside, silhouetted against the fiery glow. Earth had been saved. Again.

The credits rolled through a long list of actors, extras, and special-effects technicians.

I looked at my friend Ken sitting beside me on the couch. "What do you think?"

"Hmm," Ken said. "Cool effects. I like how the aliens sort of melted and reformed as different guys. And the exploding planetoids were awesome. But you know, it was kind of stupid too."

"Oh?"

"Yeah. I mean, in all these movies, the aliens are really awful, nasty bad guys. But with all those stars and stuff out there, maybe there're a few good aliens too. You ever think of that?"

I could feel myself smiling from deep inside. Ken was my best friend. I really wanted to tell him that I, Zack Gaither, was one of those good aliens. That I'd been planted on Earth to help when the planet would be eventually asked to join the Galactic Union. But I couldn't. It was supposed to be totally secret. I hadn't learned about it myself until a year or so ago. Even my parents had thought they'd adopted a human baby, until they'd had to learn the truth after my last mission went weird.

"Yeah," I answered carefully, "I've thought of that a lot. But enough of these lame sci-fi movies. Let's watch one of the spy thrillers we checked out."

I was just clattering through the pile of DVDs when Ken said, "I didn't know you had a cat. I thought your mother was allergic."

"Huh? We don't have a cat."

"Well that big yellow one at the window sure looks like it expects to be let in."

I looked up at the living room window. A fat yellow cat was plastered against the glass, staring intently at me with huge green eyes. I felt my skull tingling on the inside.

"Agent Zack Gaither," a voice buzzed in my mind. *"Let me in. Now! I have an urgent assignment for you. And get rid of that native youngster beside you."*

Rubbing my forehead, I tried to focus on Ken. "Er...yeah...cat. Just the neighbor's cat. Hey, before we watch anything else, I'll go see if my mom's got any cookies or something."

I got up, shot an annoyed glance at the cat and walked to the kitchen. So much for the relaxing summer Saturday with a friend.

My mother was sitting at the kitchen table sorting through a pile of papers from work. "Mom," I whispered, "I need your help with something. Alien Agent business."

Her smile turned to a worried frown. "What is it?"

"There's another agent outside. Looks like a cat. It's got some important message for me, but I can't exactly sit down and talk to a fat yellow cat while Ken's here. So I've got to come up with an excuse for sending Ken home."

She sighed. "This alien business is so unnerving, Zack. But yes, I know it's important. I'll come up with something. Give me a minute."

"Thanks, Mom. You're the greatest." And I meant it. When my dad told her a few weeks ago about all he'd learned, about his being abducted, and the aliens we'd met on that trip to New Mexico, she had believed us and said she'd support me however she could. As far as she and Dad were concerned, I was still their son, human or not.

Grabbing a bag of chips, I headed back into the living room. A minute later, Ken and I were still debating which spy movie to watch when my mom came in.

"Zack, I'm really sorry, but our plans for the afternoon have suddenly changed. I just got off the phone with your aunt Marsha. She said Paul threw out his back just now working on remodeling the attic into a den. A bunch of shingles are off, and it's predicted to rain tonight. She asked if we could come over right away and help finish the job before everything gets soaked."

I had to fight back a smile. If there's one thing Uncle Paul is *not,* it's a do-it-yourself type. He might hire expensive carpenters to remodel something, but he'd never touch a hammer himself.

"Sure, Mom. Looks like we've got to go help."

She turned to Ken. "I'm so sorry, Ken. This really spoils the fun afternoon you two had going."

He stood up. "That's okay, Mrs. Gaither. I understand. My dad's always leaving projects half-done. Drives my mom nuts."

Ken and I made plans to get together again in a few days. Then he set off to walk home.

The moment he was out of sight, a fat yellow cat bolted in the door. My mom yelped and stepped back.

"It's okay, Mom," I assured her. "It's not really a cat, just some sort of alien. You're probably not allergic to its fur."

The cat plunked itself down between us and let out a string of yowling, grating squawks. The translator in my ear tingled and then kicked in. "Get rid of this native female too," it translated. "My message can't wait."

My throat made a few attempts at speaking in the alien's language, but it hurt too much.

The cat would just have to rely on its translator while I spoke English. "Hey, this 'native female' is my mother. And she knows about all this alien stuff. So tell me the message already."

The cat snorted like a rhinoceros and yowled again, saying, "All right, but let's go to wherever you keep your doctored computer."

I turned to my mom who, of course, had understood me but not any of the cat's language.

"We're going up to my room for a minute, Mom. See, you're not sneezing yet. Looks like alien cat fur is okay."

She looked doubtful as the wide yellow cat waddled up the stairs behind me. Then she called after us. "Want me to bring up a snack? Cookies? Maybe a nice bowl of cream?"

The cat's only answer was an untranslated growl. "Later, Mom," I said. "This shouldn't take long."

As soon as I closed the bedroom door, I said to the cat, "Hey, be polite to my mom, okay? Around here, cats like cream, and you do look like a cat."

"An unfortunate coincidence," it snorted. "But that *is* why I was picked for this assignment. Been here before too." With that, it's sides seemed to expand, and I realized that its girth wasn't all fat. From out of the long fluffy hair, two leathery wings emerged. They stretched and began to flap leisurely.

Memory tickled at me. "Oh. A cat . . . with wings. Hey, were you the cat my cousin and I saved from that fierce dog when we were really little kids?"

"Saved?" it snorted. "I could have handled the brute."

"It didn't look like you were handling it so great when you were racing away from that charging Doberman."

Another snort. "Whatever. I had other priorities—you. Back then I was sent to check up on how you were doing in your adoptive home. But enough reminiscences. This is an emergency."

"So tell me."

The cat folded its wings back till they disappeared along its furry sides.

"Agent Sorn. She's been abducted. She was on her way to Earth on a routine mission when her ship was intercepted. We've traced the ship's signals here to Earth, but she has clearly been captured by the Syndicate."

"The Kiapa Kapa Syndicate?" I'd met them before. Not fun guys.

"Right. A coalition of Gnairt and other species who generally have been working against the interests of the Galactic Union. Our job, Agent Zack, is to find and free Agent Sorn, if possible. But of even higher priority is to carry out her original mission."

At that point, I had to sit down in my swivel desk chair, but my head was spinning without even one swivel. "What was her mission?"

With one paw, the cat reached into some container hidden in its fur and then handed me a shimmery blue cube. "Slip this into your computer's port. Chief Agent Zythis prepared a brief explanation."

I took the cube, inserted it, and instantly the screen filled with the image of a guy with lots of eyes and tentacles. I'd seen him before and always wished I hadn't. But *he* was supposed to be a good guy. The universe is weird.

"Agent Zack Gaither," the frothy voice said. "This could be a severe crisis. You may be familiar with the scientific project on Earth to set up radio telescopes and search for signals from extraterrestrial intelligence.

It's called SETI, I believe. Of course, this galaxy is full of intelligent species sending messages back and forth. But the Galactic Union has been deliberately jamming those messages so that Earth doesn't learn about them until it is mature enough and ready to join the galactic community. Sorn was intending to perform routine maintenance on our jamming equipment when she was abducted by the Syndicate. We don't know what their plans are, but we can safely assume they are not good." The look in all twelve of his eyes was very serious.

"Your assignment is, if possible, to find Agent Sorn and to thwart the Syndicate's plans at all costs. Agent Khh, who delivered this cube, is a species that can also pass on Earth. He will assist you. This could be a dangerous assignment, Agent Zack, but you have proved yourself before. The Galactic Union is counting on you."

With that, the friendly horror on the screen faded. All I could do for a moment was sit and stare at the blankness. Before, when these Galactic Union guys had given me an assignment, it was always with the assurance that it would be simple and perfectly safe. And they'd all turned out majorly difficult and dangerous.

This change was definitely not a good sign.

CHAPTER TWO

Agent Khh wanted me to leave immediately. But I had to talk to my parents first. And the more I thought about that, the more unsettling that was.

Now that they knew about this alien business, I could tell them the truth. I wanted to play down the "dangerous and difficult" part though. Not because they wouldn't let me go but because I didn't want them to worry.

And *that* was the unsettling part. A normal human kid might not tell his parents he was going to do something dangerous because the parents might forbid him to do it. And when you think about it, it's kind of comforting to have someone watching out for you. Though you might get mad when they said "no," at least you had an excuse for not doing something risky. At least you felt safe—thwarted but safe.

But now I wasn't a normal human kid. My parents knew I had an important job and that they really had no right to forbid me from doing it. No right to keep me safe. It was like I was suddenly a grown-up. And I didn't feel totally ready for that.

But ready or not, there I was.

My dad was home by the time Khh and I came downstairs. He had more experience with aliens than my mom, but they were both impressed by Khh's unfolding wings. The guy even flew up to the back of a chair to make a growling statement, which I translated with lots of editing. I told them how Khh and I had to go make routine alterations on some equipment and how I ought to be back in a few days. I didn't say anything about Agent Sorn being abducted or that there were bad guys involved.

Then I packed a few basics in my backpack, added the granola bars and trail mix my mom insisted I take, and we were off.

"Off" turned out to be a clump of bushes in the empty lot behind our house. That's where Khh had hidden his ship. If you have a picture of a spaceship in mind, this is definitely not it. The ship was sort of like a flying skateboard. Well, bigger maybe. A flying surfboard. It was longish and low and really small. When Khh pressed a control, the whole top lifted up like a hinged lid. Khh hopped in and scrambled up front to settle down amid a nest of controls. I crawled in after and lay on my stomach behind him. Then the lid clamped down. It was so low in there, I barely had room to crouch. I experimented, but lying flat was more comfortable than sitting hunched over.

Good thing I don't get claustrophobia. This definitely would have triggered it. Good thing I don't have a fear of heights too. When Khh twiddled some controls and the ship shot off, I realized that practically the whole thing was transparent.

Only the rim that ran around the ship's edge where the top and bottom met seemed to be solid. It glowed a dull red and must be where the power was. The rest was as clear as glass.

Above, I could see the cloud-splotched sky whipping by. Below, I could see our neighborhood, then our town, and then the country beyond. We were skimming pretty low, and I could pick out cars, cows, and everything.

"Hey, Khh," I asked after a minute. "Isn't there a danger that people will see us, flying this low?"

"None," came his translated reply. "I've set the visual deflector. That also should fool the natives' primitive radar. But if it doesn't, we're so small, we'd probably read as a large bird."

"Okay, good. So where are we going?"

"West. The tracer shows Sorn's ship has been forced down near the radio telescope site she was heading for. Our equipment there works through the human's own system, though they don't know it. It can jam extraterrestrial messages and prevent them from being picked up anywhere on this planet."

"Right. So where exactly is this place?"

Khh consulted a screen. "In some mountains near the west coast of this continent. Your info cube has more background. Now be quiet and enjoy the view."

I sighed. Kind of prickly, this cat. But the view was worth taking in. It definitely was a bird's view. Maybe one of those migrating geese. Hills and mountains rolled by under us. Rivers wriggled like snakes across the landscape. Splotches of towns appeared, passed under us, and were gone. We were sure going a lot faster than any bird or airplane.

Even though the view was fascinating, I forced myself to do the homework. Using a tiny screen set in the floor, I read more on the info cube. Then I must have slept for a while, because suddenly I jerked awake. We were going slower now and a lot lower. Cone-shaped mountains sprinkled with rocks and pines were sliding beneath us. These mountains must be fairly high, because even though it was summer, there were still patches of snow in shadowed places.

Soon we were skimming so low, Khh had us dodging gnarled trees and very solid-looking boulders. I tried not to scream and prayed that Khh had gotten straight As on his pilot exams. Only a few feet off the ground now, we wove like a bird between pitted black boulders. Then we sank and bounced over gravel into the shelter of a rocky overhang. The red rim around the ship stopped glowing, and its faint humming sound sank into silence.

The transparent lid popped open, and Khh hopped out. Stiffly, I crawled after him. I stepped cautiously from behind the big rock and was hit by a fresh chill breeze. The clear air was tangy with the faint scent of pine. Around us, a wild-looking landscape stretched in all directions. To the east, a valley was etched with a few roads, a smattering of green fields, and a cluster of white dots that might be buildings. But otherwise, it was all dark, rocky mountains furred with patches of trees. Many of the mountains had the same cone shape as the one we were on.

In the west, the horizon was rimmed with gold. The sun had just set. Above, the sky shaded from pale green to violet. I stretched, taking a deep breath of the fresh air. Khh hissed angrily from behind me.

"Get down! Our sensors show that Sorn's ship is just over that outcrop. We've got to creep close enough, without being seen, to find out what's happening."

Creeping was a lot easier for someone the size of a cat. The rough black rock covering the ground was way too sharp for me to crawl on my hands and knees. I had to walk doubled over and kept bumping into boulders and stunted trees.

Finally, Khh's bushy tail waved frantically. A signal to stop, I guessed. Good thing, since we were about twenty feet up on the edge of a cliff. I crouched down and peered around a gnarly tree trunk. The light was still fairly good, but my extra night vision had already kicked in. Useful things, these alien powers.

Below us in a hollow on the rocky mountain-side sat two obvious spaceships. One was a sort of flattened silver bubble. Sorn's, I thought. The other was much larger—and grosser. It looked like a bloated, bruise-colored octopus. Beside that bigger ship, four figures were talking. Talking rather angrily, it seemed, but we were too far away to hear what they were saying.

"Can't easily get closer," Khh muttered. "I'll send in the bug."

The thing he pulled out of a container at his side *did* look like a bug. No, maybe more like a scorpion. About three inches long, it had a segmented yellow body, lots of legs, and an upright "tail," which must have been an antenna. As soon as Khh put it on the ground, the thing skittered down the jagged face of the cliff. It was soon lost in the shadows, but already I could hear tinny voices in my ear as the bug crept closer to the alien group and transmitted directly to our implants.

"You fool, Gnairt!" a voice rasped angrily. "I should have known better than to put you in charge of the prisoner."

I shivered. I'd met Gnairt before and really, *really* disliked them. I stared at the distant figures. There were two Gnairt all right, looking sort of like fat, bald humans. But the thing yelling at them was even weirder. It was tall, pitch-black, and thin, except where it bristled about like a mangy Christmas tree. It was gesturing, and I realized the branchlike things were arms, lots of skinny arms that folded up close to its body and then snapped out and waved around. At the top of the body was something like a many-sided crystal. Its head, I guess.

One of the Gnairt was whining a reply. "It's not our fault. No one told us the Galactic Union gives its agents immunity to knock-out drugs. We thought she'd be out for hours."

Another voice hit my ear. I stared, trying to pick out the speaker and had to stifle a gasp. This was, without a doubt, the ugliest alien I'd ever seen. And I'd seen some pretty nasty ones. Think of that pretend vomit you can buy at joke stores. A flat pool of shiny stuff with puke-colored lumps scattered through it. Just my looking at it almost brought up the real thing.

When the vomit guy talked, the edges of its flat body flapped and wriggled. "If you had guarded her anyway, she couldn't have slipped out, sabotaged our ship, and escaped in the life pod."

One of the Gnairt protested and gestured vaguely to the south. "At least I got in a good shot at the pod. It's damaged and can't get far."

"We can't either!" the bristly guy screeched. "Without that agent, we can't find and take over their installation. Then the Syndicate's plan to plant false messages and eventually take over this planet will fail. And it will be your fault!" It jabbed a couple of spiky arms at the two Gnairt.

One Gnairt snorted. "So stop ranting and help us repair the ship," the other growled.

"You're always bragging what great engineers your species are. Prove it!"

The two Gnairt stomped off toward the octopus-shaped ship with the bristly alien right behind. Like a pool of sludge, the vomit guy flowed after them.

"Whoa," I breathed, as I slumped against the rock.

Khh poked my leg with a sharply clawed paw. "Move it! We've got to get to Sorn before they do."

I turned and looked at the bleak mountain-ous landscape around us. "There's an old Earth saying about finding needles in haystacks."

"So? What's a haystack?"

I pointed vaguely to the south. "Something a lot easier to look through than all of that."

CHAPTER THREE

Dizzily, Sorn clutched the controls as the stolen pod spun off to the south. That shot as she was escaping had done major damage. She struggled to keep the pod in the air and get as far away from the Syndicate crew as she could. What's more, she realized angrily, she wasn't even going the direction she wanted. But the damaged steering was sluggish, and she was dropping steadily lower.

The rough mountainous land below showed no obvious landing spots. She needed somewhere flat with a spot to conceal the pod. She hadn't had time to sabotage the Syndicate ship very thoroughly, and they could be after her soon.

The pod jerked and dropped suddenly. Wrestling with the controls, she managed to keep in the air. But clearly she'd have to land soon.

Desperately, she scanned the landscape where mountain shadows stretched long in the afternoon light. Ahead, she saw the glint of a small lake. Above it at one end was a flat plateau, not much bigger than a ledge. With the pod in this condition, it would be a tough landing. But the trail of smoke now spinning behind her made it clear there was little choice.

Sorn managed to aim the pod toward it, but she was dropping too quickly. Abruptly smoke billowed from the controls in front of her. Straining to see through it, she glimpsed the plateau coming up fast. Too fast.

Earth, Sorn realized, was rapidly becoming her least favorite planet.

CHAPTER FOUR

We stayed crouched behind the rocks until Khh's eavesdropping bug had scuttled back. Then we crept to the rocky overhang where we had hidden our little ship.

"It sounds like Sorn escaped only a little while ago," Khh said as he opened the ship and jumped in. "So there still may be an energy trace in the air. But if the pod was damaged, it might have gone down by now. We'll have to go slowly and use our eyes as well as instruments. Though it's not going to help that the sun has set."

I looked to the west. The last of the sunset had faded into purple. But behind us in the east, the sky was a hazy white. Then a glowing chink of light edged over the horizon. I smiled. I don't know about other planets, but Earth sure has a great moon.

"Full moon tonight," I said as I crawled into the ship. "That should help."

"Maybe," Khh grunted. He lowered the ship's transparent lid and slowly eased us up into the air. Keeping low, we skirted the little hollow where the Syndicate ship squatted and then we slowly glided off toward the south.

For a while, we crisscrossed over the land until Khh gave a pleased hiss. "Got it! A faint energy trail. The pod was clearly damaged. Keep a sharp eye out."

Not easy, even with my alien eyesight. The rising moon cast a crazy jigsaw of white light and inky shadow over the rough landscape. I tried not to think about Sorn down there, maybe hurt, maybe . . . No, I wouldn't think about it. She was more than my immediate boss. She'd become kind of a friend.

Our progress was painfully slow, taking hours,

but we didn't dare miss our target. The moon was moving steadily into the west. My eyes ached from staring through the ship's transparent floor. Then I saw a bright glint ahead.

"There! Something metallic, maybe." We zoomed closer. I sagged with disappointment.

"No, it's just a little lake. Moonlight on water."

Khh grunted. "But there is an energy spike there. By the lake's edge. Let's investigate."

Slowly, we circled around the lake and then slid into a landing on a small plateau above the south shore. I climbed out eagerly as soon as the lid opened but couldn't see any sign of an alien escape pod. Nothing metal anyway, but there was an odd burning smell in the chill air.

Khh had flown out and landed ahead of me. Suddenly he yipped. "Yow! Hot! Something was burning here."

I hurried over and saw a low tangle of smoldering sagebrush. In spots, embers still glowed. "Her pod crashed," I said, feeling suddenly cold and heavy.

"And skidded," Khh added. "See, scratch marks on the rock and more embers."

We followed the trail of skid marks and scorching. It was easier to see now because the eastern sky was growing lighter. Soon the sun would be up. I wasn't sure I wanted to see what it would show us.

The trail led to the edge of the plateau. There the rock and scrubs were blackened, and a few pieces of scorched metal lay around. Then I noticed scrape marks veering off at a different angle toward the rock edge. To the edge and over.

Dropping to my stomach, I peered down. The water about thirty feet below us was just taking on a milky blue in the rising light. Through it, I thought I could just make out a dark shape under a tangle of reeds. I didn't know what a Syndicate escape pod would look like, but I had a bad feeling that was it.

Khh joined me. "Not good," he muttered. "Not at all ... No wait! There's something moving down there."

I peered over again. A dark shape was climbing up toward us. I sighed with relief. "Sorn! I'll climb down and see if I can help."

"I'll be faster," Khh said as he spread his wings and flapped into the air. "I'll call if I need help."

I followed his flight down until he disappeared behind a jutting rock that also now hid the climbing figure.   In a moment, I heard a squeak and a flurry of wings as he shot back up.   Khh landed beside me, his eyes hugely wide.

"It's not Sorn!"

"Huh?"

"It's not Sorn. It's a native. A human."

"What? How..."

Khh was pacing back and forth. "We should get out of here."

I frowned.   "But maybe this person knows something."

"We can't let a native see my ship."

That made sense, but I didn't like leaving. Quickly, I peered over the edge again. I found myself staring right into the eyes of a very human-looking girl. She had red brown skin and black braids and didn't look nearly as surprised as I felt.

In moments, she had crawled up over the edge and was sitting beside me. Cooly, she looked me over and then scanned the plateau, eyes settling on our little ship where Khh had just raised the lid.

"Well, I guess that settles it," she said.

All I could do was stare at her until I finally got out, "Settles what?"

"I was down looking at that wrecked ship and couldn't decide if it was for terrorists or space aliens. But with a flying cat and another weird ship over there, I guess it's aliens."

What could I say to that? Nothing intelligent. I glanced over to where Khh was now walking very catlike toward us. But this girl had seen the wings. Then I looked back at her. "You don't seem very surprised."

She smiled slightly. "I've kind of been expecting you."

"Huh?" Another intelligent response.

"How about introductions? I'm Shasta O'Neil. My mom's mostly Wintun. My dad's mostly Irish. So who are you?"

"Eh . . . I'm Zack. And he's Khh." I didn't think I should say much more. Fortunately, Khh reached us just then and interrupted.

"Enough friendly chat," he growled in his language. "Ask her about Sorn."

"Right. Eh . . . Khh and I want to know what you saw down there. Was there anyone in the pod?"

"No, it looks empty. The pilot was taken away."

"What? Who took her?"

"I'll tell you if you tell me more about yourself."

I sighed. This was getting crazier. But there wasn't much choice. "Deal. But you first."

"I work as a volunteer guide for Lassen Park. I'd taken a couple days off to go hiking when I saw some sort of aircraft having trouble and then crash. I called it in to the park headquarters and then headed over here, though it was night by then. When I got closer, I saw someone crawl out of the wreck, a white-haired lady. She was obviously hurt, but she did the oddest thing. She shoved and dragged the little craft to the edge here and pushed it into the lake."

Made sense. Sorn trying to hide the evidence of aliens. Shasta continued. "That's about when the helicopter arrived. The lady tried to get away from it, and when they landed and came for her, she fought them off. Finally, they had to carry her on board the chopper and took off. When I finally got here, I looked around for a while and tried to put out patches of brush that were still burning. Then, once it started getting light, I climbed down to look at the ship."

For a moment, I sat there, stunned. Khh started growling, but I didn't have to wait for the translator to know what to ask. "So where would the helicopter have taken her?"

"Remember the deal? I'll tell you when you tell me who you are, who she is."

No time for a lot of lies now. We had to get to Sorn. "Okay. You're right. Sorn and Khh are aliens. I am too actually, but I grew up here. Sorn came on a mission that's really important to Earth's future, but she got captured by a bunch of majorly bad aliens, and they seem to have some bad plans for Earth. Sorn got away from them, but the little escape pod got shot, and now we've got to find her before they do."

Shasta got this faraway look on her face, and I realized that what I had just told her must have sounded like a really stupid made-up story. "Please," I begged. "I know that sounds crazy, but it's all true. You've got to believe me."

Her eyes focused on me again. "Oh, I do believe you. So I guess we've got to get to Mineral as soon as possible. That's where the park headquarters is, and the town's got a little clinic for visitors who hurt themselves hiking or skiing. Your friend was limping pretty bad."

"We?" Khh rasped. "This native is coming too?"

Shasta was already striding toward our little ship. I hurried to catch up. "Hey, you can't come along. This could be dangerous, and it's our job anyway."

She gave me her quirky little smile. "No, I've got to come. I know the area, and you guys are going to need help."

She might be right about that, but we couldn't involve an ordinary human in this. That was against all the Alien Agent rules. Of course, nothing in this assignment had followed the rule book so far. Surely not much else could go wrong.

Once again, I was really wrong about that.

CHAPTER FIVE

Still grumbling mentally, Khh stalked toward the ship, hopped in, and settled among the controls. I looked at the narrow space behind him and could feel myself blushing. "There's really not much room in this thing, so maybe you'd better..."

"No, we'll both fit." She got in and laid down on her stomach. I squeezed in beside her, trying not to brush against her, trying to think of myself as a professional Alien Agent—instead of an embarrassed kid.

The lid closed, and the power strip glowed to life. In moments, we were in the air. Beside me, Shasta gasped. "This is so cool! Flying!

Like an eagle. Like a sky spirit." Then she started giving Khh directions of how to get to the town of Mineral. He snapped that the name of the town was all the coordinates his ship needed.

We were flying low, and the view was exciting. But I couldn't keep from thinking about how easily Shasta had accepted my story. It had taken me a whole lot longer to buy into this alien stuff. Finally, as we swooped over a broad meadow, I asked, "So what did you mean, you were expecting us?"

A laugh rippled through her. "It was my grandfather. He was a Wintun medicine person. He saw things. He talked to spirits. Mostly, I thought he was a crazy old man, but I did love him. And he did have power. The things he saw often came true. When I was seven, he told me of a vision he'd had. My future, he said, was beautiful but very strange. It would twine with the star spirits. They would come and need my help. And I must help them."

Again, she laughed. "Even at age seven, I wasn't sure I believed him. But I've sort of kept looking out for star spirits anyway. And here you are!" She craned to look at me. "Though I sure didn't expect star spirits to be like you—an ordinary-looking kid and a crabby flying cat."

I shrugged as best I could in that cramped space. "I guess we were chosen because we can pass as Earth natives. I only learned I wasn't human a couple of years ago. But already I've discovered that there are some really weird-looking aliens out there."

We flew on in silence for a while. Shasta was admiring the landscape sliding under us. My mind was churning with what she had just told me. She had accepted the alien thing and was flying off with a couple of alien strangers just because an old man had claimed to have visions and believed in spirits. That was crazy!

But was it any crazier sounding than all the aliens I *knew* were out there and all their weird powers and technology? Come to think of it, why couldn't some human have mental powers that allowed him or her to glimpse the future? And if they didn't know about people living on other planets, they might as well call them spirits. Still, this whole thing had me pretty boggled.

The sight of a small town coming up snapped me out of it. A few streets of houses spread out from a minor highway. I was still nervous about this ship being seen. Even with it's high-tech, hard-to-see stuff, that glowing red power ring might draw some attention. But of the few people I saw walking about, nobody looked up and pointed.

Khh grumpily accepted Shasta's directions and put the ship down in a small clearing among a tight-packed grove of pine trees. When we climbed out, we tucked the ship beside an old log and piled fallen branches over it. Then Shasta led us through the trees until we came out behind a shed where rusty car parts poked out from stickery weeds.

"This is the town's garage and gas station," Shasta said. "My brother works here, but we ought to go right to the clinic. It's fairly new. They built it so some people could be treated without having to go to the hospitals at Chester or Birney."

We crossed the main road and soon saw a medical-looking building. As its doors closed behind us, I started feeling extra nervous. I don't like hospitals and doctors' offices. They're too clean and tidy, and the phony cheeriness they put on doesn't cover up all the hurt and fear inside. Maybe now that I know I'm really not human, it's worse because some doctor might find a sign of that.

The woman behind the front counter shot us a fake-looking smile. "May I help you?"

My tongue seemed numb, but Shasta stepped in. "We're here to see someone who was brought in a few hours ago from a small plane crash in the mountains."

"Oh? White-haired lady with no identification?"

I nodded, "My . . . Aunt Sorn."

"I'll call a doctor," she said pressing a button. Then she frowned down at Khh. "You can't bring animals into the clinic."

"Oh, but we have to," I blurted. "This is . . . her cat. Sometimes Aunt Sorn can act a bit . . . weird, but the cat calms her down."

I could see that Khh was trying to look as calming as possible, but the snarky thoughts he was shooting at me were anything but.

The receptionist gave us a doubtful look, but just then a doctor arrived, talked with her quietly a moment, and then turned to us. "So, that unidentified woman is your aunt? She was fighting so hard when our team tried to rescue her, we had to sedate her. Then she started babbling in some foreign language. Any idea what that was?"

I fought down panic. Think of somewhere so far away, no one here would recognize the language. A name popped into my mind from recent news. "She's from Uzbekistan. Originally. I mean, a long time ago." From the doctor's rather frosty expression, I wondered if I'd guessed wrong.

Did he know the language, or was Uzbekistan one of those countries the United States didn't get along with right now?

The doctor simply nodded. "Come along, and I'll check on the patient. Not the cat, though."

"The boy says it's the woman's psychological-assistance animal," the receptionist said. As Khh's annoyance fizzled in my brain, the doctor scowled and then shrugged. I picked up the "cat," and we followed him to a waiting room.

The room was decorated with framed scenic pictures of the area. Pretty maybe, if I were here being a tourist. We sat, and I picked up a magazine, pretending I wanted to read about the smiling celebrities on the cover. Then the only other person in the room was joined by a teenage boy with his wrist in a brace, and they both left.

Beside me, Shasta whispered, "What's your plan?"

I didn't have one but answered. "We'll talk to Sorn and get her out of here as fast as possible. I wish we knew how hurt she is."

Khh, sitting on the other side of me, yowled what translated as "Let's see." He reached into his fur and brought out the little listening bug. Shasta flinched at the sight of the scorpion-like thing but at least didn't do anything girlie like squeal "Eeew." Not that I'd blame her. Real scorpions are creepy. Khh set it down, and the thing scuttled across the floor and under the door where the doctor had disappeared.

Soon tinny voices sounded in my ear. "Doctor, I think you should look at these X-rays," a woman's voice said. "They're a little unusual."

"Not the only thing unusual about this patient," the doctor replied. "An unregistered flight, no identification, tried to escape the medivac team, and reportedly threw some device over a cliff once they caught her. Could have been a weapon. And now it seems she's from . . . from one of those 'stan' countries in central Asia. Looks like we should call Homeland Security on this one."

Oh great! Panic rose in me like a geyser. Why hadn't I come up with somewhere happy like an island in the South Pacific?

I turned to Shasta who, of course, hadn't heard anything sent by the bug. "Looks like we've gotten you into something really bad. You two had better go back to the ship and wait there."

"I'm not leaving . . ." she started to protest, but I cut her off.

"We might need to make a quick getaway. They think Sorn's a terrorist or something. Go on!"

Just then the door opened, and the doctor came in holding a fistful of papers. "Young man, we just have a few forms for you to fill out."

I looked at the papers he thrust at me. Lines and lines of lies I'd have to make up. Names, addresses, and medical history. I couldn't tell them any of the truth about Sorn—or me.

The doctor handed me a pen and gestured toward a table just as the nurse standing behind him screamed, "Eeek, a scorpion! Stomp on it!"

Before the doctor's foot could squash our bug, Khh pounced and made it seem to disappear. "See, how useful cats can be?" I said weakly.

Shasta and Khh quickly headed to the exit, but the doctor said gruffly, "I think you'd all better stay until this is sorted out."

"Can't," Shasta said. "The cat's acting like he's got to poop."

Khh's mental message was indignant, but I ignored him. I had more trouble than insulted space cats. In fact, I couldn't see how things could get much worse.

I was wrong, of course, as the next second showed.

"Doctor!" another nurse screeched as she ran in. "The patient is gone!"

CHAPTER SIX

Sorn forced her mind up through the drugs they'd stuck into her. She was getting plenty tired of people trying to knock her out, even though her body was trained to fight it off. She looked around the little room. Some sort of medical facility. Not good. Doctors could discover she wasn't human. And this whole stupidness was delaying her mission.

Shakily, she climbed out of bed and tested her broken leg. Still hurt, but it was self-healing nicely. She was wearing some sort of flimsy gown and didn't see any sign of her own clothes. The only personal item on a table was the wad of Earth money she'd been carrying in case of need. The Syndicate thugs had taken just about everything else, and she'd thrown her watch away when those meddling humans captured her because it was too obviously alien.

But still, she had to get out. The room had one narrow window showing some sort of tree beyond. Grabbing the money, Sorn pulled a chair beneath the window, stood on it, and fiddled with the latch. It opened easily, and in moments, she was outside standing barefoot on a carpet of dry pine needles.

She'd started limping down a narrow alley between two buildings when she saw a human coming her way. A young adult female.

"Oh, poor dear," the woman said. "What are you doing wandering around out here in a hospital gown? Did you get lost? Do you need help?"

Sorn tried to make her voice sound feeble like the old white-haired lady this person apparently thought she was. "Why yes, young lady, just let me lean on your shoulder a moment." Sorn reached up and gave the woman a nerve pinch that sent her toppling to the ground.

Sorn didn't like doing this, but clearly she couldn't walk around in this flimsy medical gown and not be noticed. Dragging the woman behind a bush, Sorn quickly exchanged clothes with her.

Before leaving the woman's purse beside her, Sorn slipped in a couple of Earth bills she hoped would cover the cost of the clothes. Then more confidently, she walked out of the alley wearing jeans, slightly too large boots and a pink tank top that said "Allison" in sparkly letters.

She looked up and down the highway. Her clothes donor would wake up in a few minutes and start yelling for help. Before that happened, Sorn knew she needed to get something to wear that hid this flashy shirt and her identifying white hair. Then she needed to find out where she was and where that was in relation to where she needed to be. Walking along the main street, she soon came to a place that might answer both needs.

The Mineral Country Store was linked to a lodge and a restaurant by a long veranda with painted tree trunks acting as pillars. On the wall outside was a large map showing "Lassen Park and Vicinity." Studying it, Sorn found what she wanted: "Hat Creek Radio Observatory." Well below it on the map was a red star on the town of Mineral saying "You Are Here." They looked annoyingly far apart, but at least she now knew where she had to go. North.

Stepping inside, Sorn grabbed a folded map from a shelf and had started looking at a rack of hooded sweatshirts when she overheard a couple of tourists talking to the woman at the counter.

"Well, we don't have a lot of time," the woman tourist said, "but we'd love to see some of the geysers and mud pots."

The sales lady smiled. "Easily done. The best batch is called Bumpass Hell, north of here on Route 89. A bit of a hike in from the parking lot but well worth it."

As the couple thanked the clerk and left, Sorn quickly grabbed a purple sweatshirt, paid for it and the map, and hurried out to find the tourist couple standing near their brown and white RV.

Limping heavily, she approached them. "Excuse me. I know this is terribly pushy of me. But I overheard that you're headed north, and I need to go that way too. I was on a hiking vacation, you see, and had an accident where I lost my pack and twisted my ankle. And now, if you could possibly give me a . . . a lift, I would greatly appreciate it."

"Why you poor thing," the man said. "Of course we can give you a lift. As far as the mud pots anyway, can't we Mabel?"

The woman cheerily agreed, and soon Sorn was sitting with them in the cab of their RV driving north out of Mineral. She was feeling a lot better about everything. Her distress call hadn't gotten through to Galactic Union Headquarters, because no one had come to help. But even on her own, she'd managed to escape the Syndicate and the too helpful humans and was now back on track to finish her mission.

And she hadn't even had to involve their local agent. Poor Zack Gaither certainly deserved some more time not having to deal with this Alien Agent business—particularly an unexpectedly dangerous assignment like this.

CHAPTER SEVEN

I hurriedly followed the others down the hall to a room. An empty room. No patient in the bed and the window open.

"That sedative should not have worn off yet!" the doctor fumed. Then he spun toward me. "Young man, I need to know more about your aunt. Fill out those forms! And someone, go out and look for her. She can't have gotten far on a broken leg."

He gave me a laser look again. "Why would she want to escape from here anyway?"

I smiled weakly. "Like I said, sir, Aunt Sorn is a little batty sometimes. Maybe she thought she was being held by . . . bad guys or something."

By now we were back in the waiting room, and I was looking down at those forms trying to think up believable lies when there was another interruption. The receptionist was leading in a young woman with bare feet and wearing only a thin hospital gown.

"This old lady," the young woman sobbed. "She looked hurt and confused and I tried to help her. But somehow she knocked me out and stole my clothes!"

"That's it!" the doctor said as he turned to the receptionist. "You already called Homeland Security?" At her nod, he continued. "Good. Now call the police."

Then he turned on me and practically stuffed the forms up my nose. "And from you, I need some answers. Now!"

"Right. Yes, sir. But first I really, really have to go to the bathroom."

He growled but pointed to a door marked "Men." Actually once I got inside, I realized

I really did have to go to the bathroom, but I was quick about it and was soon looking for a way to escape. There were two windows. One was just a narrow slit to let light in but not wide enough to let me out. The other was larger but way up near the ceiling. Still, these alien powers of mine were good for something.

Splaying my hands like a lizard's against the white tiled wall, I tried to clear my mind of everything but the need to climb. The wall was slippery and I had to start over a couple of times, but fairly soon, I was crouched on the deep window ledge trying to pry open the latch. Then came pounding on the door with the doctor yelling at me to hurry up. When I didn't answer, there was the sound of a key in the door.

The doctor stormed in, looked around, and stopped. I didn't breathe and I scrunched as far back on the window ledge as I could. He didn't look up. Then he stormed out again, slamming the door. Quickly, I flipped the latch, raised the window, and slipped out.

Running like a scared rabbit, I darted across the highway and headed around the back of the garage. Before I could plunge into the thicket of trees and head for the hidden ship, the blast of a car horn nearly made me jump out of my shoes. I turned. A battered white pickup truck was parked behind the garage. Someone was waving at me from the cab. Shasta.

"Where's your friend?" Shasta asked as I hurried over. Khh was sitting smugly beside her.

"She escaped from the clinic before I could let her know we were here. I had to escape too. They've called Homeland Security *and* the police. She stole some lady's clothes. Now she's a suspected terrorist and thief."

"This planet is crazy," Khh spat.

"No, just . . . wrong," I answered, though the craziness certainly seemed to be growing.

"So what do we do now?" Shasta asked.

I frowned. "She's probably heading north because that's where the radio telescope installation is from here. So I guess that's the direction we go too. Where's your ship, Khh?"

He flicked his tail. "In the back, under a tarp. We decided that flying it was too conspicuous at this range. So we'll use this vehicle."

"This truck? Hey, they don't let cats drive on this planet."

"I'll drive," Shasta said, obviously figuring out what we'd been saying.

"You aren't old enough, are you?"

"But I'm very mature-looking for my age," she grinned. "Don't you agree?"

I tried not to blush. Still smiling, she continued. "This is my brother's truck. He lets me drive it all the time—off the road. I'll go slow, and anyway, your friend probably won't have gone far if she's on foot."

Shasta's idea of going slow wasn't mine, particularly since in places the road was as wiggly as a drunken snake. I tried not to look scared and watched the roadside. But we didn't pass anyone looking like Sorn. She'd probably hitched a ride. After all, she looks like a harmless little old lady.

It was getting hot now, and the old pickup didn't seem to have any air-conditioning. But the country we passed through was forested at first, and it looked like it might be a nice place to go with my family for a camping vacation—if my life ever stopped being crazy. Then things started looking more and more bleak. Hillsides and meadows were half covered with tumbles of blackish red stone. It looked more like I imagined Mars or some other planet looking. Not that I remember any place other than Earth.

I'd started wondering again what my birth planet actually looked like, when Shasta reached across, switched on the truck's radio, and twisted some dials. "Police band," she said smugly. "My brother likes to know what the cops are doing and where."

I thought maybe I shouldn't ask anything about her brother, but pretty soon, we learned several interesting things from his radio. "Hey, that stolen Hummer that the police are looking for," Shasta said, "Could your friend have stolen it?"

"Maybe," I admitted. "But there was the other bulletin about looking for a white-haired lady in a pink tank top. They didn't say the two were connected."

We had just whipped around a particularly sharp curve when Shasta glanced in the rearview mirror and said, "What do you know? Hummer coming up fast."

I craned around. A huge gray Hummer was barreling up the road behind us. I squinted to see if Sorn was driving. Just as it passed us in a really dangerous spot, I realized with horror, that she wasn't.

"Your friend's not in that one," Shasta said. "Just two fat, bald guys."

My throat had gone dry. "Not just any fat, bald guys. Two Gnairt."

"Huh?"

"Two of the aliens that are after her. The others are probably in the back of that thing."

"More fat, bald guys? You know, you aliens don't look very *alien*. It's kind of disappointing."

"Well, the two others do," I answered, "and you better hope you never get to see them."

We drove on, but soon, after another glance in the rearview mirror, Shasta cut our speed. A police car with lights flashing was speeding up the road. After a breathless moment, it sped right by. Obviously, it was interested in something other than underage drivers.

"So it looks like the police are after the alien guys who must have stolen that Hummer," Shasta said. "This is getting interesting."

It got even more interesting when after another few miles of twisty road, a black sedan was seen coming up fast behind us. As it swerved past, we saw that the driver and passenger were two very ordinary-looking guys in ordinary-looking dark suits. Ordinary, except that nobody wears dark suits during a hot mountain summer.

"Your Homeland Security, I suspect," Khh growled.

"More and more interesting," Shasta said. "Looks like everyone's going to the same party."

I didn't object when Shasta poured on more speed, and it wasn't many more miles before we found out where the party was. The view was spectacular at the top of a mountain pass, but what caught our attention was a big parking lot for somewhere called Bumpass Hell. Among the parked cars was a gray Hummer, a police car, and a black sedan.

Shasta skidded into the lot and eased into a parking place. Cautiously, all three of us climbed out of the truck and looked around. There were lots of parked cars and RVs, as well as a family picnicking on a jumble of rocks and a group of Asian tourists taking pictures of one another. But we saw no Gnairt, no police, no guys in black suits—and no Sorn.

"You think all these guys are chasing your friend?" Shasta asked.

I nodded.

"Then she and the others have probably all headed down the trail to Bumpass Hell. Come on!"

Shasta sprinted off toward a trail head. Khh and I hurried to follow, but the cat's legs were too short to keep up, and there were too many people around for him to fly. So ignoring his mental protests, I picked him up and carried him.

At first we charged along a trail sketched into a mountainside, dodging around slower hikers as we caught up to them. I heard all sorts of languages as we passed and realized this place must be a big tourist draw. Then the trail started dropping steeply, and Shasta left it, heading into a clump of scraggly pines.

"I know some shortcuts. One of my uncles used to be a guide here, and I hung out in Bumpass Hell a lot."

As we swerved around boulders and skidded down dusty slopes, I managed to ask, "So what's with this Bumpass Hell name?"

"This whole place used to be one big volcano. It blew its top off a few million years ago, and its old crater is still full of geysers and mud pots. Some guy named Bumpass 'discovered' it, but he fell in and boiled off his skin or something."

That didn't sound good. And it didn't smell very good either. The breeze was carrying the stink of very old Easter eggs. We clambered over a tangle of fallen logs, and I saw where the smell was blowing from.

Below us was a huge bowl of rock, all smooth pale oranges and yellows looking like melted sherbet. Bursting out of the center were grumbling spouts of steam, simmering lakes of turquoise water, and pools of bubbling mud. The whole place was crisscrossed with raised wooden walkways with people strolling along reading placards or taking pictures.

Not everybody looked like a tourist. Gnairt, uniformed police, and guys in black suits kind of stand out. All three groups were still on the trail interspersed with regular folks. They hadn't reached the walkways yet. I scanned the people nearer the mud pots and geysers but couldn't pick out Sorn. Some of them, though, were wearing big hats and one even had a hooded sweatshirt. Hooded sweatshirt? In this heat? That woman in the

purple sweatshirt could be Sorn hiding her
bright white hair!

I pointed her out. "There, I think. We've got
to get to her before the others do."

"Follow me!" Shasta said and led us down
a steep slope in an avalanche of pebbles and
dust. Good thing we were well concealed from
the main trail, because Khh struggled out from
my arms and took to the air.

As we reached the bottom of the bowl, the air
was heated not only from the summer sun but
from the spouting steam and boiling water all
around us. I looked across this truly hellish scene
and saw the two Gnairt come to a panting halt at
the base of the official trail. The two police offi-
cers pushed past them and headed for the walkway that would eventually lead to the woman in
the purple sweatshirt. Did they know what she'd
be wearing? Maybe, because the black-suited
guys jogged off in the same direction. Shoving
aside a knot of tourists, the Gnairt followed.

"We'll cut them off!" Shasta called as she
leaped over a fence.

"But ... but what about ... ?" I sputtered, pointing at a sign with red words like *WARNING*, *THIN SURFACE*, *SCALDING TEMPERATURES*, and *DEATH*. Shasta had almost vanished behind a veil of steam before I reluctantly clambered over the rail and followed. I envied Khh's flying and cringed with every crunching step I took on the crumbly white gravel.

Hearing yelling off to our right, I guessed people were warning these crazy kids to get back on the path. But when I glanced that way, I saw a noisy tussle on one of the walkways. Gnairt may look flabby, but they're strong. One suddenly flung a police officer over the edge into a mound of powdery white ash. A black-suited guy yelled something about "more terrorists," but he had to drop his gun when the other Gnairt melted it with a blast from his own weapon.

"Hurry!" Shasta called almost invisibly from behind the steam. I followed, leaping between gaping fissures that hissed steam and coffee-colored pools that burped up big, silky bubbles of boiling mud.

Now I could see that Shasta had reached an outcrop of pale orange rock. At least it didn't look as if it was about to erupt. I hurried toward her. Suddenly the crusty ground cracked beneath my feet. I felt myself drop. Not far. But suddenly my feet felt like hot dogs dropped into boiling water.

The pain was bad but no worse than the sharp pain in my shoulders as knifelike claws dug in and lifted me into the air. After a moment's flailing, I was dropped onto warm but solid ashy ground. I knew I should thank Khh, but my shoulders hurt too much to do it properly.

Sprawling like a lizard on the ground, I looked back at the walkways. The Gnairt were lumbering forward. One turned back and with his weapon, he evaporated the walkway between them and the human pursuers. Then they advanced on Sorn. I could see it was Sorn now. The hot breeze had blown back her hood and was tangling her long white hair. She and several tourists were stranded on a dead-end branch of the walkway. They were totally surrounded by a boiling pool of milky water. Trapped.

CHAPTER EIGHT

On her stranded bit of walkway, Sorn pushed the others behind her and bravely stood between them and the advancing Gnairt. But I could see she had no weapons. Khh did, however, and flew at the Gnairt, firing something he'd pulled from under his fur. But he had to dodge blasts from the Gnairt's gun and couldn't get in a good shot of his own.

I felt helpless, lying on the ground, cut off from Sorn and her enemies by boiling water and bubbling mud. Helpless and angry. And as hot as the mud I could feel boiling furiously just under the crusty ground. The Gnairt were advancing along the walkway just above that ground now.

My mind thrust under the surface. I felt the pent up heat and rage. I embraced it. Then my mind jerked away, breaking through the crust, freeing the geyser of boiling mud.

Screams and shouts. I crawled over to the rock where Shasta was perched. Suddenly a flailing body dropped on top of me. I rolled over and looked into Sorn's startled then beaming face.

"Agent Zack! Good to see you. But Agent Khh could use a less painful technique for air-lifting people." She sat up and rubbed her gashed shoulders.

"Hey, you're rescued," the cat grumbled as he landed beside us.

"Not till we're out of here," I said and turned to Shasta. "The fastest way back to the parking lot?"

"Right!" she said, and scrambled over rocks toward a tangle of trees and thorny brush. We followed, though my boiled feet didn't enjoy pounding up the rocky hillside.

Mud spattered and breathless, we finally reached the parking lot and pelted toward our white pickup. As we passed the parked Hummer, Khh skidded to a halt and flexed open his claws. They looked a lot more like steel switchblades than ordinary cat claws. With a yowl of pleasure, he slashed into one of the Hummer's tires and raked downward.

As he sat back, surveying the damage, the Hummer's side windows suddenly opened. A vomitlike blob bulged out and slid toward him. A bristly black tree-thing shoved the blob aside and jabbed a spiky arm toward the cat. Khh spat, leaped upward, and lopped off the end of the arm with a slash of his claws. As the creature shrieked, Khh streaked toward the rest of us.

"Time to go!"

In full agreement, we all crammed ourselves into the cab of the truck. Squealing tires on asphalt, Shasta sped the pickup out of the lot. As we headed northward on the highway, she glanced over at the rest of us. I was wedged in beside Sorn, and between us sat Khh, who refused to do anything as undignified as sit in a lap.

Shasta looked back at the road and laughed shakily. "All right. I take it back. Some aliens really *do* look alien."

I laughed with her. How right she was.

"We're heading for the Hat Creek Observatory, right?" Shasta asked, her eyes shifting from the road to the rearview mirror and back again.

Sorn looked at me, "Not that I'm ungrateful for the rescue, but how is this native involved?"

"She's okay," I replied. "It's, eh, a kind of spiritual thing. Humans do that sometimes. Her grandfather kind of saw us coming or something."

Shasta grinned quickly at Sorn. "He's doing a bad job explaining. My grandpa was a medicine person, a vision seer. He once told me I needed to help star spirits when they came. It seemed crazy at the time, but I'm glad I listened to him. I've never had so much fun in my life!"

Fun? Khh and I grumbled mentally, but Sorn just smiled. "Well, we do appreciate your help, but feel free to drop out if this gets any more dangerous."

"No way!"

Sorn turned to me. "After the couple who gave me a ride stopped to see the mud pots, I thought I'd wait in the parking lot and try to hitch a ride farther north. But when the Gnairt showed up, I tried to lose them among the geysers and tourists. Didn't work too well. Good work with calling up that eruption, Zack."

I shrugged, still feeling uneasy about being able to do that sort of thing, particularly since I don't know just how I do it.

She continued. "If they didn't get boiled in mud, that flat tire should hold them for a little while. They have a general idea where I'm headed, though, and with this batch having a Tokt member, they'll have no trouble tracking us if they get close enough."

That was a species I hadn't heard of before. "Which is the Tokt?" I asked. "Are they expert trackers?"

"The other creature is a Kifth. The Tokt is the amorphous one."

"Oh, Barf Man," I said. Shasta giggled.

"Tokt may not look dangerous," Sorn said, "but they can sense life-forms and distinguish species. Even from a distance, this one should be able to sort out the auras of different creatures and at least distinguish ones that are alien to this planet. That's probably part of how they've been able to follow me."

A useful skill, I guess, but not worth it if you had to look like that.

We kept speeding around hairpin turns, but I was used to Shasta's driving by now and tried to ignore the terror. After a minute, Sorn turned to me and said, "The Syndicate pursuers I expected, but who were all the humans after me?"

"Police and Homeland Security. They think you're a crazed thief or an alien terrorist."

At her look of alarm, I added, "'Alien' as in from somewhere foreign . . . like Uzbekistan." I was glad when she didn't ask me to explain that detail. I still wished I had told the doctor Samoa or somewhere else.

Sorn shook her head, losing more strands of white hair from her frazzled ponytail. "This is getting way out of hand. Let's hope we've at least evaded the native authorities."

Not likely, I thought, since if the authorities questioned tourists in the parking lot, they could probably get a description of our truck. But I kept quiet. Sorn seemed stressed enough. Instead, I passed around granola bars from my pack and looked out the window, half-listening to Shasta's park guide comments on various landmarks.

Somewhere during her description of past volcanic eruptions, I fell asleep.

What slowly woke me was a change in motion. We'd turned off the highway, bumped over a rough road, and stopped. I blearily opened my eyes and looked around. It was almost dark. Startled, I sat up. Was it that late?

Shasta and the others were already standing outside. I scrambled out too and realized it was so dark because we and the pickup were in some sort of big shed or garage. We weren't alone, either. Several men were lifting the tarp-wrapped shape from the back of the white pickup and putting it into the back of a rusty blue pickup. Shasta seemed to be directing them.

"What . . . who . . . ?" I managed to say.

Standing beside me, Sorn said. "Your native friend is quite a find. We heard on the radio that the police were looking for our white truck. So Shasta stopped here. It's what she called a 'mobile home park.' Says her cousins run it."

Just then a man with his dark hair in a ponytail came in through the garage doors.

"A police car just cruised in. Looking for the white pickup. You and your friends better get a move on, Shasta."

"Not till they get something to eat." A big woman bustled in after him holding a large paper bag. She thrust it at Shasta and gave her a hug. "Snacks, soda, and some extra hats and T-shirts, to change your look. Now get going, sweetie."

As Sorn, Khh, and I were hustled toward the blue truck, I thanked the man with the ponytail.

"No problem," he said. "Shasta's family, so her friends are too. We'll take care of this telltale truck."

I looked and saw that they already were. A couple of the men had removed its license plate, and others were jacking it up and removing a tire. "See?" he laughed. "Why, we've been working on this old white truck for weeks. Can't be the one they're looking for."

We clambered into the cab of the blue truck and pulled on new T-shirts. Sorn had a floppy straw hat, and Shasta and I wore baseball caps. I suggested we needed a dog costume for Khh, but his reply was not one I could translate.

Within minutes we were driving slowly along the rutted roads of the trailer park. A police car was parked by the manager's building. Despite our disguises, I slumped down, but nobody stopped us as we got back on the highway and headed off north again.

Thinking about what the ponytailed man had said, I smiled at Shasta. "You sure have a lot of relatives around."

She shrugged. "For us, family is the most important unit." Then she laughed. "Of course, we don't mind saving the world either. It's just a matter of how big you define 'family.'"

That alarmed me. "Did you tell them about us?"

"No time. I just said that you were people my grandfather had once seen and told me to help. They all knew and respected him. That was enough."

We were sharing cheese sandwiches, chips, and sodas when Sorn gestured at the dashboard. "Does that dial mean that this vehicle is almost out of fuel?"

I looked. The fuel gauge definitely was in the red.

"Nah," Shasta said. "The thing's broken. Ted told me the tank was full. But couldn't Zack just mentally work the engine without any gas? He was pretty good with that mud spout."

I choked on my chips. "No way. I'm not even sure how I did that. If I tried it with a car, I'd probably blow us all up."

"Don't sell yourself short, Agent Zack," Sorn said. "You're mastering your skills nicely. And what's your Earth saying? Practice makes perfect?"

Khh snorted in my mind. "Fine. Just practice sometime when I'm not in the vehicle."

CHAPTER NINE

During that drive, another thing that helped me ignore the scary road was that Sorn made me take off my boots so she could heal my red, throbbing feet. Now *there* is a really useful alien skill. Though being able to tap into energy with my mind has its uses too. If only it came with a how-to manual.

It wasn't long before we turned off the highway where a sign pointed to "Hat Creek Radio Observatory." At first the narrow road took us by fields dotted with cows. Then the landscape became wilder with scruffy trees and brush struggling up through pitted red black rock.

"Don't park inside the observatory grounds," Sorn said. "Hide the truck as best you can among the trees outside the fence. They lock the gate at night."

Shasta managed to do that, and when we stepped out of the truck, we were hit by dry heat and silence. Khh stretched his wings and flew up to a tree. Several black-and-white birds objected loudly and shot off. I guess seeing a cat with wings must seem awfully unfair to a bird.

"This is where we'd better split up," Sorn said. "We may have lost the native authorities by changing vehicles, but the Syndicate agents know approximately where I'm headed and may be following."

"What exactly are they planning to do here?" I asked.

"From what I overheard," Sorn said, "their plan is to take over our message-jamming device and alter it to send messages of their own. They want to convince Earth authorities that the Galactic Union is an evil empire and that the Syndicate alone can protect Earth. Then once Earth accepts them as its protector, the Syndicate will exploit all Earth's natural resources and eventually enslave its people."

"Really bad dudes," Shasta said. Then she frowned. "You said that we split up here. I hope you're not thinking of keeping me safe while you three aliens go off and save the planet. This is *my* world, you know."

Sorn shook her head. "I warned you that staying with us would be dangerous. But now I need you to help, dangerous or not. I need you and Zack to stroll into the facility and play tourist. Take the tour, wander around the telescope dishes, and be visible. It'll help if you wear my purple sweatshirt with the hood up. If the Syndicate goons show up, hopefully they'll follow you while Khh and I sneak into our hidden facility and make the routine repairs."

"Decoys," I said.

"Right. Yours is actually the most dangerous job. Just keep them following you, but don't let them get too close. They shouldn't actually hurt you as long as they think Shasta is me, because they need me to lead them to the facility. That's south of here, so don't lure them in that direction. Of course, they might not show up at all, so you can just have a fun tour of the place and meet us back here later."

I've wised up enough not to trust that sort of assurance.

But I've got to admit, it was fun—at first. Shasta and I walked through the gate and up the road until we came to a big area where the trees and volcanic rock had been cleared away. What had replaced them was a staggering sight. A field of radio telescopes looking like huge white satellite dishes pointing to the sky, the blue daylight sky behind which there would be stars. I was awed and kind of choked up. The scientists who had built all this wanted so much to talk with people from those stars. And I already had—some good ones and some bad ones.

Shasta must have felt it too. She squeezed my hand and whispered, "I'm so lucky. I've actually met aliens from space." She looked at me and smiled. "And they don't *all* look like something the dog threw up. Some are almost good-looking."

I wished I didn't blush so easily. It's embarrassing to always show when you're embarrassed.

There were a half-dozen cars in the parking lot, and a group of visitors were just gathering around a young man who must be a guide. We joined them. He took us inside a low building and showed us the most elaborate bank of computers, wires, and lights I'd ever seen. Then he turned on a video about the history of the place. They'd started with one radio telescope and had now expanded into hundreds. All those dishes, day and night, were looking for messages in narrowband radio waves because those are the type they figured alien civilizations would use.

Really interesting but I had a hard time concentrating, because I kept looking at the door, worrying that a bunch of real aliens would burst in. Then the video ended, and our guide took the group outside. I scanned the area. No one creepy was lurking about, but all those telescope dishes really looked like something from a science fiction movie.

One of the other visitors asked, "How come you built this here? It's not all that high, just a few thousand feet above sea level."

The guide swept his arm around. "No, but see all those cone-shaped mountains around us? They're all dormant volcanic peaks. There's a lot of metal in volcanoes, and that helps shield us from interference from all the electronic and radio jabber coming from cities."

I was admiring that view when my throat tightened. A big gray Hummer was just driving up the road toward the parking lot.

"They're here," I whispered to Shasta. She jumped slightly and then grinned and pulled the hood of the purple sweatshirt over her dark hair. That might seem kind of odd in this baking heat, but nobody commented.

The guide said the set tour was over, but we could all wander around on our own if we wished. Some of the visitors wandered off, but most headed back to the air-conditioned building and the soft drink machine. Shasta and I walked slowly over to a big white building that looked like a giant marshmallow. The guide had said it was where they assembled each new telescope for the array. It also was very noticeable and made a brilliant backdrop for a bright purple sweatshirt.

Casually, I looked toward the parking lot. Two fat, bald guys were climbing out of the Hummer. Even from this distance, I could see that their normally pink skin was splotched with red. I suppose I should have felt more relieved that my bringing up the boiling mud hadn't killed them. I really don't like killing things. Not even flies. But the Gnairt were causing a whole lot more trouble than flies.

The Gnairt looked around. Then you could tell they'd spotted us. As they began lumbering our way, Shasta and I started drifting off among the telescopes, always avoiding going south. It's kind of scary being a decoy for hunters with really nasty weapons. But Sorn had said they'd want to capture us, not kill us. I really hoped she was right. Gnairt aren't very fast or agile. Hopefully, we could avoid even being captured.

I felt better as long as there were other tourists about taking pictures of one another with the huge dishes in the background. But one by one, they went back to their cars. Soon it was just us and the Gnairt. One was wearing a large backpack. I wondered if the vomit guy was in it. I cast a few nervous glances around. The fellow who looked like a dying tree could be out and about as well.

Shasta and I were trying to look as if we didn't notice we were being followed. But when we came to the western edge of the cleared space, I realized that if we turned back that would be harder to pull off.

While pretending to admire the view, I whispered to Shasta, "If they think you're Sorn, then they probably think you're heading to her secret installation. So maybe we should act like we're doing that. Walk into this rough country for a while and lead them on a wild-goose chase."

She grinned. "Ought to work. They don't look like very good wilderness hikers to me."

We walked forward as if we had a goal. But I soon realized that the Gnairt wouldn't be the only ones to have difficulties here. The frozen flows of lava were pitted and sharp and were sliced into by deep fissures. Smaller rocks crumbled and slid underfoot, and everywhere bushes poked up closing off any easy passage. Some of the bushes were mean and thorny. Others were like dry, white skeletons that could be snapped through but which gave no help if you grabbed at them for support.

We could hear faint grunts and crackling and knew we were being followed. We tried to speed up, but it was really rough going. Sometimes what looked like a promising route ended at a jagged fissure that had to be climbed down and then up before putting us just a few feet farther along on its other side.

At last we found ourselves in a rugged little canyon between two arms of frozen, twisted lava. We started making better time along its floor, though there were still plenty of boulders, bushes, and a few dead or dying trees to dodge.

Suddenly, one of those trees moved to block our path. Not a tree, the dark, bristly alien. Its crystal head glowed. He rasped something, and I felt thoughts of smug triumph scrabbling in my head. Then my translator picked up words.

"Enough of this. You will lead us to your installation now. Maybe then we won't kill you."

He must have thought he was talking to Agent Sorn because he was leaning toward Shasta. She stepped closer to me. "What now?" she whispered.

I looked at the rock walls on either side. Steep and sharp. No quick getaway there.

"Back the way we came!"

We turned and sprinted back down the rough canyon. The sound of hurried scrambling came from behind us. Pushing through a mass of thornbushes, we rounded a boulder and practically ran into two red-blotched and panting Gnairt. Each held really mean-looking weapons.

CHAPTER TEN

"This is horrible country you have made us chase you through," one of the Gnairt burbled. "You will lead us now, slowly, to your installation."

I heard crackling behind us and realized we had been joined by tree-man, the one Sorn had called a Kifth. I realized that though they were talking to Shasta, she couldn't understand what was being said. I spoke up. "It's still a long way from here. We didn't want to risk the natives finding it."

"Then lead us slowly." One of the Gnairt advanced on Shasta. "You have caused us so much trouble, I will have to restrain myself from killing you now."

Shasta backed away, but from behind us, one of the Kifth's bristly arms reached out and grabbed her. The hood was yanked back.

"This is not the one!" a Gnairt exclaimed.

"Bah!" the other one spat. "It is a native Earther."

Just then the backpack that the Gnairt carried bulged, and something slick and glistening started slithering out. The sound of its voice was like vomit as well. "No. I sensed alien here."

The Kifth snorted. "How can you tell? There are so many horrid species on this planet, they might all read as alien to you."

"You know nothing!" the Tokt barfed.

"Well, this is not the Galactic Union agent," said one Gnairt. "Let's kill it."

"Don't be stupid," the Kifth snapped. "They are helping the agent. They can lead us to where she is."

"They are only meddlesome natives playing us for fools." One Gnairt waved his gun at us.

"Kill them, I say!"

"There is alien here, I say!"

"Who cares? Kill them!"

"No, fool. We can use them."

All their translated arguments bounced around in my head. But I concentrated on the weapons they were waving. Energy weapons. Sometimes I'm good at energy.

The energy overload came a lot faster than I expected. One of the Gnairt howled and tried to drop his glowing, molten weapon. It landed on the other Gnairt's foot. He howled and fell over on top of the gloppy Tokt. As that one fell, he kicked the burning weapon, which brushed against the Kifth and set one of its arms afire.

We didn't stay to see any more. Ignoring the sharp lava rock slicing our hands, Shasta and I scrabbled up the side of the little canyon and flung ourselves over the top before a weapon blast from below shattered the rock behind us and burst a clump of dead bushes into flame.

"Follow them!" came a cry from one Gnairt.

"Don't bother," said the other. "My shot must have killed them."

"Fool," screeched the Kifth. "We need them."

"We don't," burped the Tokt. "Alien, maybe, but not the right alien. I stretch my senses and feel that the agent we seek is south of here. These were decoys."

Shasta and I lay perfectly still while the aliens below squabbled but eventually moved away. The brushfire around us had burned itself out when we raised our heads and looked over the rocky ridge. The Syndicate thugs were heading south.

Shasta looked at me. "That thing that happened with the exploding gun. Did you do that?"

If I hadn't already been so flushed with desert heat, I would have blushed again. "Yeah, I guess."

She smiled. "Impressive."

We followed the aliens or tried to. The terrain was the same nightmare—frozen flows of jagged lava sprinkled with prickly brush and cut into by crevasses. The sun was near to setting, crossing everything with tricky shadows. We tried to keep them in sight but worried about being seen. The easiest one to see was the tall Kifth, but I didn't know how his eyes worked, whether he could see behind him or not. We tried to stay out of sight as much of possible, but that meant we kept losing sight of our quarry.

At least we could tell we were heading south because the tall conical peak of Mount Lassen, still streaked with snow, was ahead of us. But there was lots of rough territory between us and it. I wished I had Khh's ship, which could follow energy traces, because their recently fired weapons would surely leave them.

That thought stopped me dead. How was I so sure of that? Because . . . because I felt them! Like a faint whiff of smoke trailing after them, the alien energy they carried left a hazy trace in the air. I didn't know how long it would last, though.

"I think I can follow their trail even without seeing them," I told Shasta. "But we've got to hurry and keep up."

She looked at me but didn't say anything. I was glad. I kind of wished she saw me as a regular kid instead of as an alien with superpowers.

I sure wasn't the master of those powers, though. When I tried too hard, I almost lost the trace. But I found that if I sort of let my mind go all fuzzy, it was as if I were a dog following the scent of a big meaty bone.

Daylight was fading fast, making it even harder to clamber through the lava field. I was nearly exhausted when suddenly I felt a change. The energy trace was no longer blowing in the air in front of us. It had sunk down.

I looked around. The ground here was cleft into several short, rugged canyons. The sinking whiff of energy pulled me down into one. Wending our way through the rocks and brush on its floor, we rounded a ragged boulder. What had looked like a dead end suddenly wasn't. A jagged, dark slash gaped in the rocky wall.

Cautiously, I stuck my head in and felt a hint of energy. Slipping off my backpack, I fumbled inside for my flashlight. "You got a flashlight too?" I asked Shasta.

She unclipped something from her belt. "What sort of guide-in-training would I be if I didn't?"

The opening wasn't large, but we squeezed our way in. I hoped the Gnairt and the others had found it even harder. We flipped on our lights and flashed them around. Large rocks were piled up with only a narrow passage between them. If this was a cave, it had almost totally been blocked by a big rockfall. Then we were passed the rocks, and the cave suddenly opened up. In the crisscrossing beams of our lights, it looked like a big smooth-walled tube vanishing into the darkness. To me, it also looked like the throat of some gigantic serpent. A throat about to swallow us up.

Not a comforting thought.

"Cool!" Shasta whispered. "A lava tube. There are supposed to be hundreds of these in the Lassen area, but people have only found and mapped a few of them. They were formed by molten lava rushing underground."

We walked cautiously at first, but though the surface was uneven, the way was clear. That ancient river of red-hot lava had cleaned things out pretty well.

"Of course," Shasta continued, "in the old days, we Wintun had a different explanation for these places. They were the homes of dark spirits. Ones described as looking sort of like Bigfoot."

I groaned. Bad enough that we were dealing with alien would-be invaders. I didn't want to face the—hopefully—mythical Bigfoot too.

Usually caves are cool, and a cool cave would have been welcome after the heat outside. But soon I noticed that I wasn't feeling much cooler. In fact, I was sweating. But I was still following the energy trace, and that's what

I concentrated on. The tunnel wound like a snake but was wide and easy to follow.

Then there was a branching to the right. The main tunnel clearly went to the left, but I felt the energy trailing into the side channel. There was more rock rubble in the floor here, and the winding channel was lower and narrower. It was also a dead end.

We played our flashlights over the rough wall at the end. No openings. Yet that's where the energy trace led. I stepped around a rubble pile, looking for some way through. Nothing on the wall, but there at the base of a boulder was a dark opening, a cleft in the cave floor.

Dropping to my knees, I shone my light into the darkness. It wasn't a straight drop like a well. The passage slanted, and chunks of lava formed a rough staircase. I could feel the energy trace flowing down it.

I didn't know how far away the others were, so I was afraid to talk. I pointed to the hole, Shasta nodded, and we started down. It was awkward climbing down, holding a flashlight in one hand, and I was afraid the light might give us away. I had to keep it on, though, because my alien night vision wasn't good in total darkness and we wouldn't be much help if we fell and broke our necks.

After twenty or thirty feet, the slanting passage ended in a jagged cleft. I flicked off my light and cautiously stepped out with Shasta right behind me. There were no lights or voices, so we switched on our lights again.

Shasta gasped. "Wow! A second lava tube underneath the first. That's something new."

This tunnel did look a lot like the last, but it was even hotter. Our cleft had opened in the wall of a tunnel that ran in both directions. The energy trace seemed to glisten in my senses like a snail train, and it led to the right.

We followed it to where the tunnel branched again and once again took the turn to the right. This narrower channel wound slowly downward into the darkness. Several side channels slanted off, but the energy trace led straight ahead. I was trying to move as silently as possible, but suddenly I tripped over something and toppled forward, sending my flashlight clattering over the rocky floor.

I froze waiting to hear some reaction to the noise—a shout or weapons fire maybe. Nothing. No, there was a muffled thumping and my mind sizzled with a voice.

"Clumsy near-native! Now that you've kicked me, get me out of this!"

CHAPTER ELEVEN

Behind me, Shasta shone her light on the thing I'd tripped over. A bundle of slimy stuff. I peered at it. Glaring from inside the nearly transparent slime were two angry eyes. Cat eyes.

"Khh! How did you . . . "

"*I was standing guard,*" came the answer in my head. "*There was a fight. That disgusting Tokt spewed this over me. Now get me out!*"

Shasta didn't need my translation to see the problem. She immediately had a knife out and began carefully gutting the stuff away. It was like half-hardened snot and was totally gross.

When he was finally freed, Khh shook himself harder than a wet dog.

"Yetch! Now, move. They'll have Sorn trapped in the equipment chamber. Hurry!"

We did hurry, and soon I heard voices above the thumping of our feet. Loud voices from people obviously not listening for anyone coming. There was also a faint glow of light coming down the twisting passage.

My translator implant tingled. "You might as well cooperate," said a Gnairt. "Surely it's not worth losing your life for the sake of this backward planet."

Sorn's response was cold. "I am an agent of the Galactic Union, and my job is to protect planets like this."

"No point in protecting them from the Syndicate," came the raspy voice of the Kifth. "We've wanted this planet for some time, and we'll take it before your slow-acting Union gets around to doing a thing. All we need is instructions on how to tap into your equipment so we can send these native fools some messages of our own. Then you can go free and return to your precious Galactic Union with the message that Earth is off their do-gooding agenda."

The burpy voice of the Tokt followed. "Or you can *not* tell us how to work it, we kill you, figure it out anyway, and the Union still loses."

All through this, the three of us had been creeping closer. The tunnel was steadily getting hotter. Light was seeping around a bend, and the voices came from just ahead.

I switched off my light and risked peering around the rocky corner. The tunnel ended in a good-sized chamber. One wall of it was lined with very alien-looking equipment. Sorn sat in front of it tied to a chair. The others were clustered around her with their back to us. One Gnairt was waving his gun around.

Briefly, Sorn seemed to glance our way, and then quickly, she looked back at the tall Kifth, who had to bend over to fit under the low ceiling.

"This equipment is very delicate. It uses thermal energy, which is quite close to the surface here," Sorn said evenly. "I'm not sure you can master it without a lot of training. But in no circumstances should you use that weapon in this room. Even though *it's the only weapon any of you have now,* its use could set off a bad reaction, which I doubt you could control."

The Kifth began protesting that they had vast technical knowledge, but I didn't listen. Sorn's message was clear. Only one weapon.

Khh got the message too. *"Charge!"* he yelled in my head. Flapping his wings, he shot into the room, heading straight for the Gnairt with the gun. I followed and tackled the other Gnairt like a football player. I was afraid to use any energy tricks, because Sorn might not have been lying about that.

I got a glimpse of Shasta heading toward the captive Sorn, but my attention was diverted by sight of the tall Kifth swiping at me with one of his bristly arms. I rolled the Gnairt I'd tackled into him like a bowling ball, and he toppled over, smack into the Tokt. But the vomit guy just reared up, flipped them off, and launched at me like a mad flying carpet. I had visions of being engulfed in snot just as Khh had been.

But it never happened.

Shasta must have managed to cut Sorn free from the chair, because a chair came flying through the air just then and smacked into the Tokt, veering him off course and smashing him into some of the machinery. He slid to the floor in a shower of sparks.

Sorn and Shasta were at the chamber's entrance. Between me and them was a major battle. Khh had been fighting with the Gnairt for control of the gun. That Gnairt was riddled with deep cat scratches, but now the other had come to his aid, trying to pry the cat off his fellow Gnairt's arm. The tall Kifth had managed to get back on what passed for his feet. Before I could reach them, the creature had slashed down with a spiny arm, peeled off Khh, and slammed him against the rock wall.

Khh yowled but leaped up in time to dodge a blast from the Gnairt's gun. The energy beam smashed into the wall, filling the room with rock and dust.

And something more. A low grumbling, which I had thought was Sorn's machinery, suddenly became louder. And the cave room was also much hotter and brighter. Brighter with red, glowing lava.

Sprinting for the entrance, I didn't look back but raced after Shasta and Khh up the slanting tunnel. I heard shouts and screams behind me and other running feet. But none of those guys were built for speed.

Then from behind came the sound of cracking like falling rock. But whatever was happening didn't seem to stop the advance of the lava. The red glow was following us. So were the horrible alien screams.

I wasn't sure even we could outrun that stuff.

Khh was in the lead and must have had the same thought. "Quick, in here! There's a side tunnel."

The flying cat swooped into a narrower tunnel that slanted more sharply upward. Sorn, Shasta, and then I followed. The heat was intense and the climb steep and made more difficult by the rock rubble that seemed to cover the floor. Now I could see the red glow at the entrance of our little side tunnel. And behind the light came the lava. Most of it would probably stay in the main tunnel, but some of it was climbing after us. If we could just make a dam.

Loose rocks were everywhere. The only energy source I had with me was my battery watch. Desperately, my mind reached into the little disk, grabbed the power, and thrust it at the small rocks lying up and down the tunnel.

The effect was an avalanche that knocked me off my feet. I grabbed at a crack in the rock wall and kept from being swept down into the rising lava. Something slammed into me, and I just managed to catch Shasta's arm before she was swept by. We huddled together, pelted by rocks.

Our flashlights had been swept away, but the angry glow from below showed us Sorn clinging to a jutting rock just behind us. Khh was flapping madly to stay above the avalanche.

We all coughed in the settling dust. The tunnel was dimmer than moments before. I staggered to my feet and looked back. Rocks covered the dome of lava like nuts on a cheese ball. Weird, the images your mind comes up with.

Largely feeling our way, we continued climbing. I tried furiously not to think that this might be a dead end. But the more I ignored it, the more the fear gnawed at my skull. There certainly was no way back.

"At least it's less hot now," I said to Shasta in case she was half as scared as I was. "We'll be out in no time."

"Of course, we will. Don't you feel that breeze?"

"Huh?" Then I did feel it. A tiny trickle of cool air was fluttering down the tunnel. There was even a faint mist of light. A few more steps and the gray light was enough to make

out Shasta's face. That face was filthy with
dust and sweat, but it was split by a wide grin.

"You know, hanging around with you space
guys is even more exciting than in the movies."

CHAPTER TWELVE

Even with Earth's wonderful full moon, it took a couple of hours to make our way over the old lava fields to where we had hidden the pickup. I kept worrying that the ground would suddenly burst open in a fiery gusher or that a massive earthquake would knock us off our feet. But the night stayed quiet except for some rasping insects, a few night birds, and the distant cry of a coyote.

Both Sorn and Shasta thought the unleashed lava would probably stay in the lower tube and harden fairly quickly. Apparently the heat energy from that lava, when it was safely behind the rock wall, was part of the power Sorn had used to operate her device.

Just the same, when we got to the pickup, Sorn wanted to head east for a ways so we could drive up the rim that formed the side of Hat Creek Valley. She wanted to keep an eye on things for a while.

"Enough has gone wrong on this assignment," she said as our truck lumbered out from behind the dark screen of pines, "that I just want to be sure I'm not also responsible for radically changing this volcanic landscape yet again."

Once we had zigzagged our way to the top of the rim, we parked the truck and settled ourselves among a pile of boulders to look over the valley below. The moonlight gave it a misty unreality. Desolate landscape surrounded a clearing that was sprinkled with white telescope dishes, their faces turned hopefully to the stars. Even with the bright moon, there were a lot of bright, beautiful stars.

"So what happens now?" I asked Sorn.

She sighed. "Not what we had wanted. The Syndicate's plot is thwarted, but so are our plans. With our jamming equipment destroyed, it won't be long before those telescopes start picking up extraterrestrial messages. Then humans will learn that they aren't alone in this universe. That could cause mass panic or at least tremendous worry and confusion. So the Galactic Union will have to step up its timetable, reveal itself, and invite Earth to join."

Sorn turned to look at me, her tangled white hair glowing in the moonlight. "And you know what that means to you, don't you Agent Zack?"

I swallowed. "It means going into the Alien Agent business full-time."

She nodded. "I had so hoped you'd get a chance to grow up, complete your training, and still enjoy a relatively normal Earth life. But now, sooner than you should, you'll have to take up your role as envoy between the Galactic Union and the people of Earth."

Sitting on the other side of me, Shasta punched my shoulder. "Don't look so gloomy, Zack. You can do it. You've been pretty extraordinarily great these last two days."

I looked at her. "Thanks. But sometimes just being ordinary is nicer."

"Well, you can have that for a while longer," Sorn reassured me. "It could be some time before those telescopes pick up any alien messages, and it's certain to take a while to get Earth's invitation approved by the Galactic Union Council."

"Yeah," Khh said from the gnarled pine he'd perched on. "You can look forward to months and months of being a boring human kid. Honestly, I don't see the attraction."

"Hey," I objected. "Don't knock this planet. It's a good place."

"It is," Sorn agreed as she gestured at the valley below us. "And one of the things that proves it is down there. Curiosity, hope, ingenuity. That's what those radio telescopes stand for. Humans want to find and be part of something bigger. They're born adventurers."

At that, Shasta stood up. "We are. But it's time I dropped out of this adventure—just for a while, mind you. I've got a couple of borrowed trucks to return. Then I've got to get back to my volunteer guide work at the park."

I stood up too, hesitated a moment, and then gave her a hug. I'm pretty sure the moonlight didn't betray my blush. "You've been a really great guide all right. And a big help. Thanks for believing my crazy story."

"Hey, it's my story too, remember? And I doubt it's over yet. My grandfather said the star spirits would be part of my future. And I'm counting on having a lot of future left."

Shasta helped us unload Khh's ship from the back of the pickup. Then, after more farewells, she drove back down the twisting road. I watched her, feeling oddly lonely. There weren't any other human kids who knew and weren't afraid of what I was.

Khh's paw swiped my ankle. "Come on, kid. Back to work."

"That cat has about as much sentiment in him as a rock," Sorn laughed. "But it looks like things are going to stay stable down there. So now we've got to go collect my ship and destroy the Syndicate ship, so some humans don't find it and freak out. Then I'm back to headquarters, and you're back home for a while."

Home. That sounded good.

It wasn't long before the three of us had crammed into Khh's flying surfboard and were flying over the valley. Below us, the array of telescopes kept up their hopeful search. Yes, I wanted to go home, but I suspected the definition of "home" was soon going to change for me.

I took a deep breath and suddenly felt very happy.

Ready or not, universe, here I come!

alien
envoy

pamela F. Service
illustrated by mike gorman

TOP SECRET
from
ALIEN ENVOY

DOWNLOADING....

The school gym was decorated with orange and black streamers and the usual Halloween cardboard cutouts: black cats, pumpkins, and such. The planning committee had divided the gym floor into areas for apple bobbing, pin the tail on the unicorn (some of the girls on the committee had insisted), and a haunted house. The place was noisy with kids and music.

I kind of wanted to try the spook house but thought it might be lame. Ken and I decided to just stand outside and look smug until someone we trusted came out and said it was cool. We watched the dancing at one end of the gym. Finally, Ken said, "Want to dance?"

"With you?" I squeaked.

"No way! No, I mean there's a bunch of girls standing over there. Maybe we ought to ask someone."

He sputtered into silence. I prodded him a little.

"You really want to?"

He grinned. "No. Forget it. I really can't think of any girl I'd like to dance with."

I couldn't either. Well, I had met a girl this last summer who might be kind of a fun dancing partner. But she lived miles and miles away and was probably at another Halloween party with her own friends.

Getting more and more bored, I scanned the crowd and suddenly froze. Hey—I was supposed to have alien powers, not a genie's. But there was the very girl I'd just thought about. Shasta O'Neil. It was impossible. And yet the closer she walked toward me—straight toward me—the more it looked like her. Black braids, bronze skin, a trouble-making glint in her eye.

"Zack! I hardly recognized you in your dashing pirate outfit." She grabbed my hand. "But thank the spirits we found you!"

I stared at her a moment, turning as red as a fire engine. Then her words clicked. "We?" I managed to say. "Who else is . . . ?"

My eyes moved across the room and picked out the white hair and purple skin of Agent Sorn as she pushed her way through the crowd. Agent Khh was perched on her shoulder, his wings tucked into his long fur.

"What . . . ? Why . . . ?"

By then Sorn had reached me.

"Agent Zack. We must leave immediately. You're in danger."

about the author

Pamela F. Service has written more than twenty books in the science fiction, fantasy, and nonfiction genres. After working as a history museum curator for many years in Indiana, she became the director of a museum in Eureka, California, where she lives with her husband and cats. She is also active in community theater, politics, and beachcombing.